P9-DDS-839

Until We Got Princess

written by
Rob Thomas

illustrated by
Margie Chellew

MONDO

First published in the United States of America in 1995 by
MONDO Publishing
By arrangement with MULTIMEDIA INTERNATIONAL (UK) LTD

Text copyright © 1988 by Robbie Thomas

Illustrations copyright © 1988 by Multimedia International (UK) Ltd

All rights reserved.

No part of this publication may be reproduced, except in the case of
quotation for articles or reviews, or stored in any retrieval system,
or transmitted in any form or by any means, electronic, mechanical,
photocopying, recording, or otherwise, without written permission from
the publisher. For information regarding permission contact MONDO
Publishing, One Plaza Road, Greenvale, New York 11548.

Printed in Hong Kong by South China Printing Co. (1988) Ltd.

First Mondo printing, July 1995

99 00 01   9 8 7 6 5

ISBN 1-57255-052-X

Originally published in Australia in 1988 by Horwitz Publications Pty Ltd

Original development by Robert Andersen & Associates and Snowball Educational

Friends used to like coming to our house...

until we got Princess.

We used to have a clean and tidy house...

until we got Princess.

Our neighbors used to like us...

until we got Princess.

We used to be able to sleep at night...

until we got Princess.

Rob used to have a big, fluffy teddy bear...

until we got Princess.

Mom used to have beautiful shoes…

until we got Princess.

14   "Do something, or that dog must go!" warned Mom.

So Rob trained her.
Then everyone was happy, even Princess...

until we got Prince!